Shannon
the Ocean
Fairy

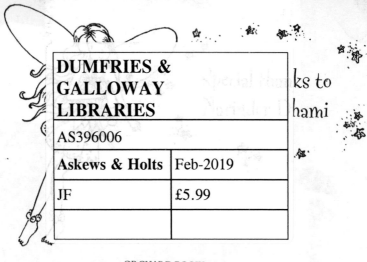

DUMFRIES & GALLOWAY LIBRARIES	
AS396006	
Askews & Holts	Feb-2019
JF	£5.99

ORCHARD BOOKS

First published in Great Britain in 2013 by The Watts Publishing Group
This revised edition published in 2019 by The Watts Publishing Group

1 3 5 7 9 10 8 6 4 2

© 2013, 2019 Rainbow Magic Limited.
© 2013, 2019 HIT Entertainment Limited.
Illustrations © Orchard Books 2013, 2019

A CIP catalogue record for this book is available from the British Library.

ISBN 978 1 40835 963 1

Printed and bound in Great Britain by CPI Group (UK) Ltd, Croydon, CR0 4YY

MIX
Paper from
responsible sources
FSC® C104740

The paper and board used in this book are made from wood from responsible sources

Orchard Books
An imprint of Hachette Children's Group
Part of The Watts Publishing Group Limited
Carmelite House, 50 Victoria Embankment, London EC4Y 0DZ

An Hachette UK Company
www.hachette.co.uk
www.hachettechildrens.co.uk

Shannon
the Ocean
Fairy

by Daisy Meadows

ORCHARD

www.rainbowmagicbooks.co.uk

Contents

Story One:
The Dawn Pearl

Story Two:
The Twilight Pearl

Story Three:
The Moon Pearl

Jack Frost's Spell

To the palace we will go,
Because my spell will make it so.
Enchanted Pearls I mean to take,
Leaving chaos in my wake.

Tides will rise to flood both worlds,
While my goblins have the pearls.
So goblins keep them safe for me
Hidden deep beneath the sea.

Story One
The Dawn Pearl

Chapter One
Party in Fairyland

"Race you to that rock pool, Kirsty!"
Rachel Walker yelled to her best friend,
Kirsty Tate.

"You're on!" Kirsty replied.

Laughing, the two girls raced across
the beach. Rachel reached the pool first,
but Kirsty was right behind her.

"Your gran's lucky to live in Leamouth," Rachel panted, gazing around the sandy bay. "It's lovely."

Kirsty nodded. Leamouth was a pretty fishing village with winding streets and a harbour filled with boats. Kirsty's gran lived in one of the cottages on the cliff, near the beach.

"I always have fun here," said Kirsty. "I'm glad you could come too, this time."

"Thanks for inviting me," Rachel replied.

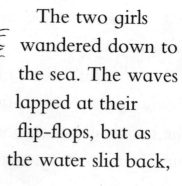

The two girls wandered down to the sea. The waves lapped at their flip-flops, but as the water slid back,

it left a large seashell
on the sand, right
in front of them.

Rachel picked
it up. "It's
beautiful," she
said. "Look!"

As Kirsty looked,
a burst of aquamarine sparkles suddenly
fizzed out of the shell, making Rachel
jump.

"Fairy magic!" Kirsty gasped.

The girls glanced excitedly at each
other. Their friendship with the fairies
was a very special secret.

The faint tinkle of bells and soft music
floated out of the shell. Quickly, Rachel
held it up so that she and Kirsty could
listen.

"Hello, girls," said a silvery voice.

Rachel grinned at Kirsty. "It's the Fairy Queen!" she exclaimed.

"We'd like to invite you to a special beach party — a luau — to celebrate summer," the queen went on. "We get together with all our ocean animal friends, including the fairies' best friends, the narwhals. If you'd like to come, just place the shell on the sand, right now.

We hope you can join us ..." The queen's voice faded away. With a quick glance around to make sure nobody was watching, Rachel placed the seashell on the sand. Immediately, a dazzling rainbow sprang from the shell, its colours bright in the sunshine.

"Let's go, Kirsty!" Rachel whispered.

Kirsty nodded, and the girls stepped on to the rainbow. As soon as they did so, they were whisked away in a whirl of fairy magic.

When the sparkles vanished, the girls realised that they had been magically

transformed into fairies and were now in
Fairyland, standing on a beautiful sandy
beach next to a glittering turquoise sea.
The beach was crowded with fairies
enjoying the luau, and the sea was
full of magical ocean animals. Kirsty
in Rachel gazed in awe as they saw
a magnificent narwhal leap out of the
water. It flipped in midair before landing
again with a graceful splash.

As the girls stepped off the rainbow,
their fairy friends rushed to greet them,

including King Oberon
and Queen Titania.
"We're so glad you
could come, girls," said the
King kindly.

"A party wouldn't
be the same without you," the queen
added.

"Thank you for inviting us," Rachel
and Kirsty chorused.

"Come and boogie!" called Jade the
Disco Fairy.

Laughing, Rachel and
Kirsty started dancing with
Jade. Meanwhile, they could
see Melodie the Music Fairy
conducting the musicians, and
other fairies making drinks and
cooking food on a barbecue.

"The tide's coming in," Rachel remarked to Jade as the waves crept further up the beach. "Will the party be over soon?"

Jade shook her head. "No, we're fine as long as we stay above Party Rock," she replied, pointing to a large boulder next to them. "But Shannon the Ocean Fairy can explain it better than I can."

A nearby fairy turned and smiled at the girls. She wore a peachy-pink skirt, a top of aquamarine ribbons and a glittering starfish clip in her hair.

"Hi, girls," said Shannon. "Jade's right. The sea never comes in beyond Party Rock, so we and our ocean

animal friends can enjoy the party all
day long!"

"Great!" Rachel said happily.

A little while later, the girls were
having fun dancing with their fairy
friends when the music suddenly
stopped. Everyone turned to see
what had happened.

"Listen, please," called Shannon the
Ocean Fairy. "I'm afraid that the sea's
coming in too far!"

She pointed her wand at Party Rock
and everyone gasped in surprise. The
water was splashing around the base
of the rock, and the level was still rising!

"The water never comes in this
far," Shannon declared anxiously.
"Something's wrong!"

Chapter Two
High Tide

King Oberon frowned. "Maybe Jack Frost is up to mischief again," he said.

Queen Titania nodded and turned to Rachel and Kirsty. "Girls, would you come back to the palace with us?" she asked. "You might be able to help."

"Of course we will," Kirsty and

Rachel replied immediately. Whenever Jack Frost and his goblins caused trouble in Fairyland, the girls helped the fairies put things right.

"And I'll explore my underwater world and see if I can find out why the sea is rising," Shannon said, jumping into the water alongside the narwhal and giving it a hug. She took its fin in her hand, and together they dived neatly under the surface. Quickly, the other fairies began to clear the beach. Meanwhile, the king and queen led Rachel and Kirsty back to the Fairyland Palace.

"We'll go to the Royal Observatory,"

King Oberon said. "It's at the top of the tallest tower. The roof slides back so that our telescopes can view the night sky."

"And Cedric, our Royal Astronomer, guards the Enchanted Pearls there," Queen Titania said as they climbed the spiral staircase. "The pearls are magical, and very important in Fairyland and in your human world."

"Why?" Kirsty asked.

"The rosy-pink Dawn Pearl makes sure that dawn comes each morning so that the day can begin," the queen explained. "And it also affects the levels of water in the oceans."

"The silver Twilight Pearl makes sure that night falls every evening," the King added. "And the final pearl is the creamy-white Moon Pearl. It controls the flow of water through the oceans and the size of the waves." He sighed. "I think something is wrong with the Dawn Pearl, and that's why the sea is coming in so far. It will disrupt the lives of all the ocean animals – including our special friends, the narwhals."

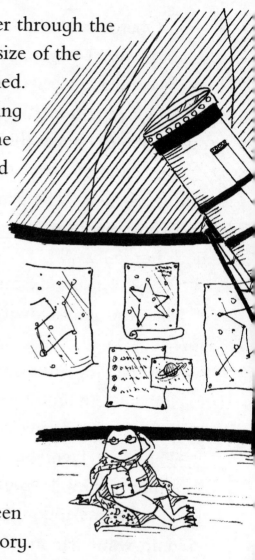

Rachel and Kirsty followed the king and queen into the observatory.

The room was painted white, but the sliding roof, which was closed, was a deep blue like the night sky. There was a large golden telescope, and star charts hung on the walls.

"Cedric!" Queen Titania exclaimed, and the girls suddenly noticed a frog footman sitting on the floor, looking rather dazed. He was wrapped in a long velvet cloak embroidered with moons and stars.

"What happened?" asked the

queen, hurrying over to him. "Are you all right?"

Cedric looked very upset. He pointed to a crystal box that was lying open on the floor. "Jack Frost and his goblins have stolen the Enchanted Pearls!" he told the queen sadly.

"What?" King Oberon exclaimed, horrified.

"Jack Frost again!" Kirsty whispered to Rachel.

"Let's see exactly what happened," said Queen Titania, and she pointed her wand upwards.

As magic from the queen's wand streamed across the ceiling, images

began to appear. There
was Cedric, studying a large
chart, when a blast of wind
suddenly swept the door
open and in burst Jack Frost
and a group of goblins.

Shocked, Cedric leapt
to his feet, but Jack Frost
pointed his wand at
him. Immediately an icy
breeze shot towards the
footman, whirling
his cloak around him
and tying him up in knots.

"Help!" Cedric cried, as a fold of the cloak wrapped itself firmly around his head.

Jack Frost smirked at him. "Quickly, get the Enchanted Pearls!" he shouted to his gang of goblins.

While Cedric struggled with his cloak, three goblins rushed over to the crystal box, flung back the lid and grabbed the large, gleaming pearls inside: one pink, one white and one silver. Throwing the box carelessly to the floor, the goblins held the pearls up triumphantly.

Jack Frost looked very pleased. "This serves those horrible fairies right!" he cried. "The king and queen banned me from the luau because I haven't been behaving myself. Well, without the Enchanted Pearls, their beach party will be a washout!"

He laughed spitefully. "There's going to be mayhem in the fairy and human worlds with these pearls missing. Time and tides, daybreak and nightfall – all will be disrupted!"

29

"Great idea, master!" said one of the goblins. "Where shall we hide the pearls?"

"I'm fed up with the fairies always finding the magic objects we steal," Jack Frost said, thoughtfully. "So, this time, we will hide the pearls in the human world – but underwater!"

The goblins looked terrified. "But we can't breathe underwater," they moaned.

"Fools!" Jack Frost said scornfully. "My magic will soon sort that out."

He pointed his wand at the goblins and a stream of large, icy bubbles flew from its end. Each bubble floated down over one of the goblins' heads like an old-fashioned diving helmet.

"Now you can breathe underwater,"

Jack Frost said. "And these …" he went on, aiming his wand at the goblins' big green feet, "will make you super-speedy swimmers."

A burst of frosty sparkles swirled around the goblins' feet and, suddenly, they were all wearing huge black flippers.

Jack Frost looked sternly at the goblins. "Now, keep those Enchanted Pearls safe, or you'll have me to answer to!" he snapped. And, with another wave of his wand, a freezing wind sprang up

and swept the goblins straight out of the window with the Enchanted Pearls.

Chapter Three
Underwater World

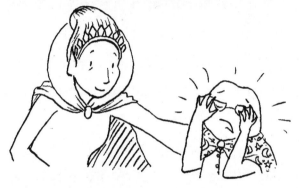

"I'm sorry," Cedric said, as the pictures faded away.

"It's not your fault, Cedric," Queen Titania said gently.

"We must summon Shannon and tell her what has happened," King Oberon declared, waving his wand.

Seconds later, Shannon fluttered into the observatory. "Your Majesties," she gasped, "my underwater world is in chaos! All the tides are wrong and it's upsetting the sea creatures."

"That's not surprising," King Oberon said grimly. "Jack Frost has stolen the three Enchanted Pearls and sent his goblins to hide them in the ocean in the human world."

Shannon looked horrified. "But that's going to affect the seas and daytime and night-time in the human world and in Fairyland!" she cried.

The queen nodded. "It's up to you, Shannon," she said. "Do you think you can get the pearls back?"

"I'll do my best," Shannon replied.

"We'll help," Rachel said eagerly.

"Won't we, Kirsty?"

"Of course," Kirsty agreed, "except that we can't breathe underwater."

Shannon grinned. "No problem, girls!"

She raised her wand and the girls saw two shiny bubbles stream towards them. They felt the bubbles settle over their heads, and then they heard a POP as the bubbles disappeared.

"Now you can breathe underwater," Shannon announced. "Let's go. There

isn't a moment to lose!"

"Good luck," the queen called as
Shannon lifted her wand again. "And
remember that the Enchanted Pearls will
be much bigger in the human world!"

As magic sparkles from Shannon's
wand cascaded down around them,
Rachel and Kirsty shut their eyes.

"Welcome to my underwater world,"
Shannon laughed a moment later.

The girls opened their eyes. To their
amazement, they were standing on the
sandy golden seabed, surrounded by
large shells and pink coral. A crowd
of narwhals bobbed alongside them,

waving their
fins happily in
greeting. "We're
under the sea!"
Kirsty cried, and then
clapped her hand to her
mouth in astonishment.
She was breathing and
talking normally, as if she was
on land. Strangely, the water didn't
seem to feel wet, either.

"It's magical!" Rachel agreed.

Suddenly, the narwhals came together
in unison and started to swirl around

each other. The water around them rippled in the most beautiful spirals and shapes. The girls watched in amazement.

"That's the special Dance of the Narwhal," Shannon explained. "It brings luck to anyone who is fortunate enough to see it."

Then she put her head on one side, listening carefully.

The girls listened too and heard a strange barking sound, which gradually got louder and louder.

"Ah, now here are some friends who will help us find the goblins!" Shannon exclaimed happily, and, a moment later, a pack of sea lions came racing through the water.

"Hello!" Shannon called.

The girls watched as the sea lions bounced playfully around Shannon, chattering and barking loudly.

"Follow me!" Shannon called.

She darted off and Rachel and Kirsty followed. As they whizzed through the warm water, Kirsty was fascinated by the shoals of fish and the inky coral caves.

"The sea lions told me the goblins are near this shipwreck site," Shannon said, pointing at the remains of a Spanish galleon on the sea floor. "It's a very popular place for divers, so we must find the goblins before someone spots them!"

Rachel gasped as a woman's figure

loomed up in front of her. "Oh, it's a ship's figurehead!" she said, touching the peeling paint.

Just then, Kirsty's eye was caught by a

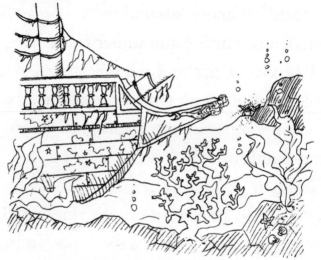

glint of gold on the seabed.

"That's a gold coin!" she said excitedly, pointing. "Look how brightly it's shining. There's lots of light around here."

"I know why that is," Shannon

replied. "This isn't
normal sunlight. It's the
magical dazzle of the
Dawn Pearl!"

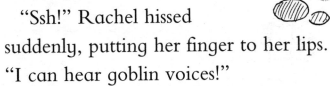

"Ssh!" Rachel hissed
suddenly, putting her finger to her lips.
"I can hear goblin voices!"

Shannon, Rachel and Kirsty quickly
swam behind a rock and then peeped
out cautiously.

A moment later, three goblins came
swimming towards them – and one was
carrying the Dawn Pearl.

Chapter Four
A Treasure Trail

Rachel and Kirsty caught their breath as they gazed at the pearl. It was a beautiful rose-pink colour, and it shone with a dazzling brightness that filled the ocean with light.

Shannon and the girls watched as the goblins suddenly shot forward, their magic flippers propelling them quickly through the water.

"They're very fast swimmers with those flippers," Shannon whispered.

"We won't be able to catch them if we have to give chase!"

The goblins began to swim around the wreck of the Spanish galleon, holding the pearl out in front of them.

"They're using the pearl like a torch!" Shannon frowned. "I hope none of

the human divers around here spot
the light."

"The goblins are looking for
something," whispered Kirsty.

"There's no treasure here!" the biggest
goblin exclaimed in disgust. "Let's look
somewhere else."

The goblins moved away from the
galleon and along the seabed. Shannon
and the girls followed.

"Look, a treasure chest!" the smallest
goblin squealed,
pointing at a
tarnished silver chest,
half-buried in the sand.
He swam down and
heaved the lid back.
Then he gave a shriek
of fear as a shoal of

brightly coloured fish swam out.

The other goblins roared with laughter. Shannon grinned too, but then her face fell. "Oh, no!" she cried. "Girls, this is terrible!"

Rachel and Kirsty looked puzzled.

"Do you see that cleft in the rocks over there?" Shannon whispered, pointing at a narrow opening in a nearby rock wall.

The cleft was surrounded by vibrant blue and green seaweed and amazingly bright pink sea anemones.

"That's the entrance to the Mermaid Kingdom," Shannon went on.

"You mean, mermaids are real?" Rachel gasped.

"Yes, but they're very secretive," Shannon explained. "They're scared of being discovered by humans and having their kingdom revealed. Imagine the fuss!"

Rachel and Kirsty gazed in wonder at the narrow rocky pass, now lit brightly by the Dawn Pearl.

"If any divers come along now, they'll spot the goblins and maybe find the Mermaid Kingdom, too!" Shannon said anxiously.

Kirsty glanced at the goblins.
Suddenly an idea popped into her head.
"Maybe we can lure the goblins away
with some treasure!" she exclaimed.
"If you could magic up some gold coins,
Shannon, we could lay a trail for the
goblins to follow."

"I can do that," Shannon agreed.
"The magic coins won't last for ever,
but they should stay long enough to fool
the silly goblins."

"We could trap them in one of the coral caves we saw on the way here," Kirsty went on.

"Good idea," Rachel said eagerly. "With the goblins trapped, maybe we can get the Dawn Pearl back."

"And I know just how we can trap them!" Shannon declared eagerly. "I'll be back in a moment, girls."

And, with that, she swam quickly away, returning a few seconds later. "I've asked some friends for help," she explained, winking at the girls. "Now, let me magic up a trail of gold!"

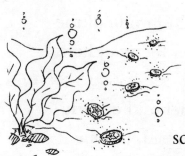

She waved her wand and the girls saw a trail of shiny coins appear in the sand, leading into a nearby coral cave.

"I hope the goblins spot them," Shannon whispered as the three friends hid inside the Spanish galleon.

The goblins were still swinging the Dawn Pearl this way and that, searching for treasure. Suddenly, one of the goblins gave a shriek of triumph as he spotted

a coin glinting in the sand.

"Treasure!" he yelled, scooping it up.

Shannon and the girls grinned at each other.

"I see another one!" the biggest goblin shouted, dashing forward to grab a second coin.

Shannon, Rachel and Kirsty swam silently after the excited goblins as they picked up the gold coins, one by one. Kirsty held her breath as the goblins paused outside the cave.

Would they go in?

Chapter Five
In the Coral Cave

To Kirsty's relief, the goblins hurried inside the coral cave.

"Let's go!" Shannon whispered, and she and the girls swam over to the cave mouth. Inside, the goblins were scrabbling around on the sandy floor, looking for more coins.

Shannon cleared her throat loudly. The goblins shrieked with surprise.

"Please give me the Dawn Pearl," Shannon said politely.

"No way!" the goblins snorted.

"We're not letting you leave until you do," Rachel told them.

"You silly little fairies can't stop us!" the biggest goblin declared, moving defiantly towards the girls, followed by his friends.

Just as the girls were wondering what to do, they heard a swishing sound.

Looking down, they saw the narwhals gliding into the cave and swiping at the goblins with their tusks. The goblins screeched in dismay and backed away.

"We can't stop you," Shannon agreed, "but my narwhal friends can. And they'll keep poking you if you don't give back the Dawn Pearl."

The goblins looked annoyed, but they screamed in fear when the narwhals moved towards them again.

"OK," said the biggest goblin. "It's yours!"

The goblins tossed the Dawn Pearl across the cave and Shannon, Rachel and Kirsty caught it between them.

"Thank you," Shannon called. "And thank you, my narwhal friends." She waved her wand and a burst of fairy dust swept Rachel and Kirsty out of the water in an instant. Blinking as

the magic dust cleared, the girls realised that they were back on the beach in Leamouth.

"And we're

not even wet," Kirsty said, looking down at her dry clothes.

"That's fairy magic!" Shannon laughed. She tapped the tip of her wand on the Dawn Pearl and it immediately shrank to its Fairyland size. Then another sparkling shower of fairy dust made Kirsty and Rachel return to their normal sizes once again.

"I must take the Dawn Pearl back to Fairyland now," Shannon said. "Thank you for all your help, but we still have a difficult task ahead of us. We must find the other two Enchanted Pearls!"

Rachel and Kirsty nodded and waved.

Their fairy friend
blew them a
kiss, and then
disappeared with
the Dawn Pearl
in a whirl of fairy
magic.

Story Two
The Twilight Pearl

Chapter Six
Ship Ahoy

"It's another gorgeous day, Rachel!" said Kirsty. "What shall we do?"

It was the following morning, and the girls were getting ready to go out with Kirsty's gran.

"I don't mind," Rachel replied. She glanced across at Gran, who was tidying the kitchen, and lowered her voice. "Maybe we helped to make the day start so bright and sunny by finding the Dawn Pearl."

"Maybe," Kirsty agreed. "I just hope we get a chance to help Shannon look for the other missing pearls today."

"What about a walk to the pier this morning, girls?" Gran suggested.

"That's a great idea!" Kirsty exclaimed. "There's a fairground at the end of the pier with a rollercoaster ride that goes right out over the sea!"

"Ooh, fun!" Rachel said with a grin.

Gran laughed. "Come on, then,"
she said.

They all set off along the seafront
towards the pier.

"Look at that big cruiseliner out at
sea," Gran remarked, as they passed
the harbour.

Rachel and Kirsty looked out across
the water to see a huge white ship with
black funnels in the distance.

"I don't suppose it will be stopping at Leamouth," Gran went on. "Those big ships never dock here."

"Look, Rachel,

there's the old lighthouse," Kirsty said. "There are some really dangerous rocks around the harbour, so the lighthouse was built to guide ships in safely."

Rachel stared up at the white-and-red-painted lighthouse standing on a rocky outcrop at the harbour entrance. "Is it still working?" she asked.

Gran shook her head. "No, modern ships have all sorts of high-tech equipment to guide them these days," she replied. "There are plans to turn the lighthouse into an artists' studio."

They walked on towards the pier, at the other end of the beach.

"I expect you girls want to explore," Gran said as they reached the entrance. "I'll have a drink in the café while I'm waiting for you."

Gran led the way to the Starfish Café, a little way along the pier, and sat down at a table looking out over the sea.

"A pot of tea for one, please," Gran told the waiter.

The man wrote it on his notepad.

"See that big cruiseliner out there?" he said chattily. "It's called *Seafarer*, and they've just said on the local radio station that it's going to dock right here in Leamouth!"

"Really?" Gran asked, looking surprised. "That's unusual."

"Yes, apparently the ship is having problems with its navigation systems and so it needs to dock as soon as possible," the man explained. "You'll have a perfect view of it from this table, although it won't be docking for an hour or so yet."

"It'll be brilliant to see the ship coming in," Rachel commented.

Gran checked her watch. "Well, why don't you go and explore, and then come back to watch the ship dock?" she suggested. "I'll sit here and read till you get back," she added, taking a book out of her handbag.

"See you later then, Gran," said Kirsty, and she and Rachel set off together along the pier.

"The sky looks very black over there by the harbour entrance, even though

the sun's shining," Rachel remarked, pointing far out to sea.

Kirsty nodded. "Maybe there's a storm coming," she replied.

The girls were just passing a small games arcade, when a machine by the entrance started flashing its lights and playing a merry tune.

Rachel stopped. "'FREE PLAY'," she read aloud from the little screen.

"Have a go!" Kirsty urged.

"I've tried this before but I'm no good at it," Rachel admitted.

The machine was full of soft toys in a glass case, and a large metal claw hung above them.

The claw, which was used to grab the toys, was operated by a lever. Rachel took hold of the lever and moved the claw downwards. It swung around a bit, but Rachel finally managed to grab a fluffy narwhal toy.

"Well done!" Kirsty cried, as Rachel carefully moved the narwhal over to the chute and released the metal claw. The narwhal dropped straight down the chute.

"You did it!" Kirsty laughed.

Smiling, Rachel drew

back the panel to retrieve her prize,
then gasped as a cloud of aquamarine
sparkles burst out.

"Hello, girls!" Shannon the Ocean
Fairy cried. "I need your help to find
the Twilight Pearl – and fast!"

Chapter Seven
Narwhals in the Night

Rachel and Kirsty were keen to help.

"You'll have to be fairy-sized," Shannon said. "Quick, get out of sight."

Rachel and Kirsty ducked swiftly behind the machine, where one flick of Shannon's wand transformed them into little fairies, complete with glittering wings.

Once again, Shannon conjured
up magic bubbles to enable the girls
to breathe underwater.

"Let's go, girls," Shannon said,
flying off towards the end of the pier.

Rachel and Kirsty whizzed after her.

"Nightfall is already being disrupted in
parts of the world because the Twilight
Pearl is missing," Shannon explained as
they flew. "Last night, darkness didn't
fall at the South Pole – luckily, only the

penguins noticed!"

"There aren't any people living at the South Pole, are there?" asked Rachel.

"No, there aren't," Shannon replied, "so no humans have noticed the disruption yet. But if the Twilight Pearl isn't restored to its proper place soon, there'll be night-time chaos everywhere!"

"Where are the goblins with the Twilight Pearl?" Kirsty asked.

"I think they're underwater somewhere near here," Shannon replied. "The presence of the Twilight Pearl is causing darkness to fall near the entrance to Leamouth Harbour."

77

"So that's why it's so dark!" Rachel said, as they reached the end of the pier. "We thought there was a storm coming."

"Follow me!" Shannon called as she plunged downwards into the sparkling blue sea.

Rachel and Kirsty dived beneath the waves after her. As they sank deeper, the sun filtered down through the water, lighting up the golden seabed and rippling fronds of seaweed. A shoal of silvery fish flickered past them and the girls grinned in delight.

"This way," Shannon said, darting through the greeny-blue water.

Rachel and Kirsty followed until Shannon stopped and turned to them.

"Look, girls," she said, "can you see how the colour of the sea is changing?"

Rachel and Kirsty gazed ahead of them. Sure enough, the greeny-blue colour of the water was deepening to a dark indigo.

"This is the

effect of the Twilight Pearl," Shannon explained. "It's becoming night-time everywhere."

She tapped her wand lightly on her hand, caught a sparkle as it fell and then fixed it to the tip of her wand, where it glowed brightly. "We'll use this to light our way. I just hope the goblins don't spot us coming."

Shannon swam off more slowly this time, with Kirsty and Rachel close behind her. But although Shannon's glowing wand helped a little, the waters around them were steadily growing

darker and darker.
Kirsty wondered
how they were
ever going to find
the goblins and the
Twilight Pearl in the
ever-increasing gloom.

Suddenly, Shannon stopped again,
tipping her head to one side and
listening. "We need the narwhals again,"
she said, looking determined. "Wait
here, and I'll be back in two shakes
of a fish's tail!" And she shot off into the
darkness.

Rachel and Kirsty
waited hopefully.

Seconds later,
Shannon came back.
"Here they come,"

she announced, holding up her lighted
wand. Rachel and Kirsty gasped as,
behind Shannon, they saw the
narwhals up close for the
first time.

"They are so
beautiful," whispered
Rachel.
The narwhals
swam around the
fairies, squeaking
and clicking in
greeting, glimmering
beams of light shining
out of their tusks.

"The narwhals know
the oceans better than
anyone else," Shannon explained.
"They're going to take us to the

goblins." She waved her sparkling wand. "And they have offered to let us ride on their backs, so we'll get there even more quickly!"

"That's fantastic!" Rachel exclaimed.

"I can't believe it," Kirsty breathed as one narwhal swam over to her and squeaked, inviting her to climb aboard. Kirsty clambered carefully on to its sleek back, as Rachel and Shannon jumped on to their own narwhals.

"Make sure you hold on tight," Shannon called, grabbing on to

her narwhal. "When a narwhal swims
fast, it's really fast!"

"I see what you mean!" Kirsty gasped,
as her narwhal took off like a rocket.

Chattering happily to each other,
the other narwhals followed. Rachel
and Kirsty hung on tightly as they
zipped through the darkening seas.

"This is fun!" Rachel called.
"Woohoo!" she cheered as her narwhal

leapt out of the water and glided through the air in a perfect arc before plunging beneath the waves again.

Soon it was so dark underwater that Shannon and the girls could hardly even see each other, but the narwhals were still sure of where they were going, so neither Rachel nor Kirsty felt scared.

Suddenly, the narwhals began to slow down. In the darkness, the girls could

hear voices ahead. They exchanged
a knowing glance.

"Goblins!" whispered Kirsty.

Chapter Eight
Grumbling Goblins

The narwhals began to circle the goblins while Shannon, Kirsty and Rachel kept very still, listening hard. The goblins sounded scared.

"Oh, I don't like the dark," one whimpered. "Eek! What was that?"

"Maybe it was a sea monster,"

another moaned. "I can't see."

"Something just swam past me," cried a third. "And I think it was an underwater Pogwurzel!"

"HELP!" all the goblins shouted. "WE'RE LOST IN THE DARK!"

Rachel and Kirsty could dimly see Shannon fixing another sparkle to her wand. It fizzed like a firework, lighting up the ocean around them.

The goblins stared
in amazement
at the circling
narwhals.

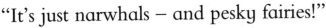

"It's not a
Pogwurzel," one
goblin sneered.
"It's just narwhals – and pesky fairies!"

"Give the Twilight Pearl back,
and we'll rescue you from the dark,"
Shannon offered. "We know you're
scared."

"Rubbish!" the biggest goblin scoffed.
"We're not scared, and we're certainly
not giving back the pearl."

"OK, we'll go – and
I'll take my light
with me," Shannon
said firmly.

"NO!" all the goblins shrieked at once.
"Please stay," gabbled the biggest
goblin, looking terrified. "But we can't
give the pearl back."

"Why not?" asked
Rachel.

"Well, it's just that
…" the big goblin
said hesitantly.

"We hid the pearl
somewhere really
safe," another
goblin added.

"And now we can't find it!" said
another, sheepishly.

"But we know it's under a really big
rock," added the big goblin helpfully.

Shannon whipped her wand through
the water. It briefly lit up the sea around

them before fading away.

In that time, Rachel and Kirsty saw that the area was full of really big rocks!

Suddenly there was the booming sound of a ship's horn overhead. The goblins cried out with fear and

clapped their hands
over their ears.

"I think that must
be the *Seafarer*'s
horn," said Rachel. "It's
coming to dock in Leamouth because
its navigation systems aren't working
properly."

Shannon turned pale. "The *Seafarer*
won't be able to find its way through
the rocks in the darkness caused by the
missing Twilight Pearl!" she exclaimed.

"It might run aground!"

Rachel and Kirsty
glanced at each other
in horror.

Then Kirsty's gaze
fell on the glowing
tip of Shannon's wand

92

and an idea took shape in her mind.

"The ship would be OK if it had a light to guide it, wouldn't it?" she pointed out. "Shannon, could your magic get the old lighthouse working again?"

Shannon looked excited. "I think it could," she said. "But we'll have to hurry." She glanced at the goblins.
"Stay here and keep out of trouble!" she told them.
"When I get the lighthouse working, you'll have some light down here."

93

She jumped off her narwhal, patted its nose and then zoomed up towards the surface.

Rachel and Kirsty said a quick goodbye to their narwhals and followed.

They broke through the water and
shot up into the air, then gasped
in amazement.

The Twilight Pearl had made night
fall, and the sky around them was
velvety black and spangled with stars
that sparkled like diamonds. It was
beautiful.

"There's the *Seafarer*," Kirsty shouted,

pointing at the faint silhouette of the ship near the harbour entrance.

"And look at all those rocks in its path!" Rachel added anxiously.

Chapter Nine
A Light in the Dark

"To the lighthouse, girls!" Shannon cried. She whizzed off at great speed through the blackness, and the girls zoomed after her.

"How are we going to get inside?" Rachel asked when they reached the lighthouse door, which was locked.

"There's a broken windowpane there," Shannon said, pointing upwards.

She led the way up to the window and into the dark lighthouse. It smelt dusty and damp as the fairies flew up the spiral staircase to the very top of the tower. There was the huge lantern, surrounded by

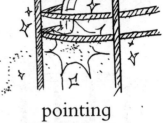

mirrors to reflect the light out to sea.

"Look, the bulb's broken!" Rachel exclaimed, pointing at the lantern. "The electricity has probably been switched off, anyway," said Kirsty. "It hasn't been used in years."

"My fairy magic can fix it," Shannon replied, pointing her wand at the lantern. "But my spell won't last for ever. I just hope it's long enough for the *Seafarer* to dock safely."

Rachel and Kirsty watched as a stream

of sparkles flew from Shannon's wand and surrounded the lantern.

With many loud creaks and groans, the lantern began to turn. Slowly, too, the broken bulb began to glow, getting brighter and brighter.

"It's lighting up the sea for miles!" Kirsty cheered. "Look, it's showing up all the rocks around the harbour mouth."

As the three friends watched, the *Seafarer* began to make its way

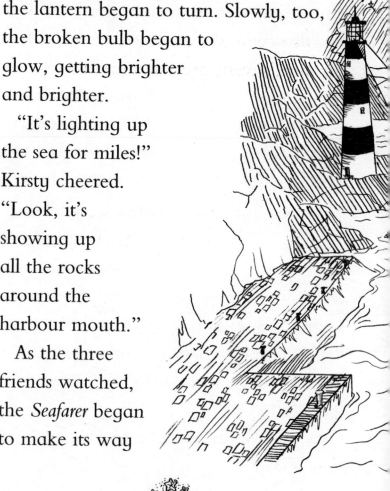

into the harbour.

And then Rachel noticed something
odd: every time the lantern's
beam fell on a particular place
in the ocean, she could see a
strange, silvery-grey shimmer in
the water.

"Thank goodness," said Shannon,
once the *Seafarer* had cleared the
rocks.

"Now we'd better see
what those naughty goblins
are up to."

She zoomed over to the window and Kirsty followed.

But Rachel hesitated, waiting for the light to fall on the same patch of water once more.

"Shannon, look over there!" Rachel cried, pointing as the sea glittered silvery-grey. "Could the Twilight Pearl be there, underwater?"

Shannon looked where Rachel was pointing and then clapped her hands in delight. "It *is* the Twilight Pearl, I'm sure of it!" she declared.

"Well done, Rachel," Kirsty added. "Let's get it!"

Swiftly, the three friends whizzed out of the lighthouse, heading straight towards the glittering patch of sea.

As they plunged down into the deep water, they were bathed in an eerie silver light that shimmered all around them.

"There it is!" Kirsty exclaimed, spotting the Twilight Pearl lying beneath a large rock. She gazed at it in wonder. The pearl's unusual, silvery sheen was truly magical.

But suddenly, to Kirsty's horror, a

goblin swam sneakily round from the
other side of the rock and grabbed the
Twilight Pearl!

Chapter Ten
From Twilight to Sunshine

As Shannon and the girls watched in dismay, all the other goblins appeared.

"Oh no," Rachel groaned. "The beam from the lighthouse has helped the goblins find the pearl, too!"

"We'll have that, please," said Kirsty, holding out her hands. But the goblins just laughed.

"Go away!" jeered one. "The pearl belongs to us!"

"If you don't give us that pearl right now," Shannon said, looking very fierce, "I'll turn the lighthouse off again and leave you here. You know how Pogwurzels love the dark!" And she winked at the girls.

The goblins looked panic-stricken. "Take the pearl. Take the pearl!" they gabbled, pushing it through the water to the fairies and swimming speedily away.

Laughing, Shannon touched her

wand to the Twilight Pearl. It shrank
immediately, and she swept it up into
her arms, spinning round in delight.

"Everyone in Fairyland will be so

pleased to have the
Twilight Pearl returned,"
she cried. "But, girls,
you must get back to
Kirsty's gran so that you
can watch the *Seafarer*
come into dock."

The three friends flew
quickly to the deserted
end of the pier, where
Shannon soon restored
Kirsty and Rachel to their human size.

"We just have the Moon Pearl to find
now," Shannon reminded the girls as she
gave them a quick hug. "See you again

very soon!" And she
vanished in a cloud
of fairy dust.

Rachel and
Kirsty hurried
back down the
pier. As they passed
the arcade, Kirsty

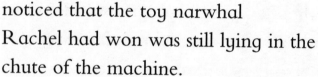

noticed that the toy narwhal
Rachel had won was still lying in the
chute of the machine.

"Look, here's your narwhal," Kirsty said, handing it to Rachel.

"Let's share it," Rachel suggested. "It'll remind us of our fantastic underwater adventures!"

Kirsty nodded and the girls ran back to the café, where lots of people had gathered to watch the *Seafarer* approach.

"Ah, there you are, girls," said Gran. "I was worried a storm was brewing; it was so dark out at sea. But luckily someone's managed to get the old lighthouse working to guide the *Seafarer* in." Rachel and Kirsty shared a secret smile.

The huge cruiseliner was

moving slowly into the harbour now. As
it did so, the darkness began to lift and
the sun came out. Everyone clapped and
cheered as the ship docked safely.

"Look, the lighthouse is dark again
now," Kirsty whispered. "Shannon's
fairy magic kept it working just long
enough!"

"And the Twilight Pearl is safely back
in Fairyland," Rachel added happily.

"Now, I wonder where the goblins have hidden the Moon Pearl ..."

Story Three
The Moon Pearl

Chapter Eleven
Message in a Bottle

"Oh dear!" Gran exclaimed as she read the paper.

"What's the matter, Gran?" asked Kirsty. It was the following morning, and the girls were getting ready to go down to the beach.

"There are reports of major floods

in coastal areas all around the world," Gran explained. "Apparently the sea is behaving very strangely, and the high tides are coming in much further than they usually do."

Rachel and Kirsty glanced at each other in concern. They knew that this was because the Moon Pearl, which controlled the tides, was missing from Fairyland.

"Have fun at the beach, girls, but make sure you're back for lunch," Gran went on. "And just keep an eye out for the tides, although Leamouth doesn't seem too badly affected at the moment."

"OK," the girls agreed.

"I wonder if Shannon's found out where the goblins are hiding with the Moon Pearl," Rachel said as they hurried through the garden and down the cliff steps to the beach.

"I hope she has," Kirsty replied. "All those floods sound scary!"

It was still early so the beach was deserted. The girls decided to go straight down to the sea and paddle. Removing their flip-flops, they waded into the cool, clear water.

"Isn't it funny to think we were

actually under the sea yesterday?"
Kirsty remarked.

Rachel was about to reply when her
eye was caught by a green glass bottle
bobbing up and down on the waves.
It had a cork in the top, and, with
a rush of excitement,
Rachel realised that
there was a piece
of paper inside.
"Kirsty, look at
this," she called,
grabbing the bottle
as it floated past
her. "It's a message
in a bottle."

Kirsty paddled over and peered
through the glass at the piece of paper.
"It says 'Open me!'" she said.

Rachel smiled broadly. "Let's see what happens," she said, pulling out the cork.

Immediately, a sparkling mist of aquamarine dust burst out of the bottle – and so did Shannon the Ocean Fairy!

Chapter Twelve
Flooding in Fairyland

"Girls, I need your help!" Shannon declared, looking very pale. "Fairyland is flooding fast!"

"Oh no!" Rachel exclaimed.

"Is everyone safe?" Kirsty asked.

Shannon shook her head. "The toadstool houses are being flooded,"

she explained. "Fairyland is in chaos!"

"How can we help?" asked Rachel.

"We must find the Moon Pearl without delay," Shannon replied. "And I think I know where the goblins who have it are hiding."

"Where?" asked Rachel.

"Hawaii!" Shannon told her.

"Hawaii?" Kirsty repeated, amazed. "How are we going to get there?"

"With fairy magic, of course!" Shannon laughed. Quickly she waved her wand and turned the girls into sparkling fairies. Once she had conjured up some magic bubbles too, so that the girls could breathe underwater, they were ready to go.

"Follow me," Shannon said, diving neatly into the waves.

Kirsty and Rachel did the same.

"Now, stay very close to me," Shannon instructed, linking arms with the girls and waving her wand again.

Rachel and Kirsty let out a gasp as they were suddenly swept off their feet at top speed. The three friends were

carried through the water by a magic
current, their hair streaming out
behind them.

They were going so fast that the girls
couldn't see anything except for swirls of
rainbow-coloured bubbles that were also
swept along on the stream of magic.

A few minutes later the girls felt
themselves slowing down.

"That was like a super-fast
rollercoaster ride!" Rachel exclaimed

in delight as she caught her breath.

Kirsty nodded. "The water feels much warmer here," she remarked.

"That's because we're in Hawaii," Shannon declared. "See the coral reef?"

Rachel and Kirsty gazed around. The sea was a clear sapphire blue and there were all kinds of colourful tropical fish weaving their way through the reef of pink, red and white coral. The sun shone through the water, creating pretty

patterns on the seabed.

"It's like an underwater garden," Kirsty breathed.

"Let's go and see what the goblins are up to," Shannon said with a grin. "I think they're up here." She zoomed upwards and the girls followed.

Peeping out of the water, Rachel and Kirsty saw a beautiful island nearby with palm trees and a golden, sandy beach.

"Listen," Shannon whispered.

Rachel and Kirsty suddenly realised that they could hear shouts and whoops of glee. They turned and saw a big, rolling wave making its way towards the beach. And riding on top of the

wave, on brightly coloured surfboards,
was a group of giggling goblins.

Chapter Thirteen
Weird Waves

Rachel, Kirsty and Shannon had to muffle their laughter as they watched the goblins surfing. They all had garlands of flowers around their necks and some were wearing flowery Hawaiian shirts or long grass skirts.

"They look so funny!" Rachel

laughed. "But aren't they supposed to be in hiding with the Moon Pearl?"

"I think they've forgotten about that," Shannon replied. "They're having so much fun!"

"These waves are enormous," Kirsty remarked as another huge wall of water headed towards the beach. "They're perfect for surfing."

Shannon nodded. "Yes, that's what Hawaii's famous for," she said. "But these waves are even bigger than usual!"

She frowned. "I think the goblins are using the Moon Pearl to make the waves bigger. And to do that, they must have the Moon Pearl underwater and close at hand."

"Let's start searching!" Kirsty said eagerly.

The others nodded and the three friends ducked under the water again.

As Rachel and Kirsty looked around for any sign of the Moon Pearl, they suddenly spotted a group of tiny, bright blue narwhals bobbing through the water towards them.

The narwhals swam right up to them.
These ones had beautiful, delicate flower
garlands along their tusks.

They squealed and clicked at the
fairies.

"They are so beautiful," Kirsty said.
"I wonder what they're saying."

Shannon grinned and waved her wand,

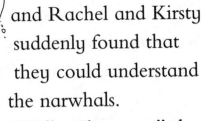

and Rachel and Kirsty
suddenly found that
they could understand
the narwhals.

"Hello, Shannon," they
chorused. "Hello, girls."

"We're very pleased to meet you,"
said one.

"Yes, very pleased to meet you," the
others repeated.

Rachel and Kirsty were enchanted.
"We're very pleased to meet you, too,"
they replied.

"These young Hawaiian narwhals are friends of mine," Shannon explained. "I've known them ever since they were born."

"Yes, ever since we were born!" the narwhals chorused in agreement.

"Ever since we were born!" squeaked another one, a little behind his friends.

"We're looking for the Moon Pearl," Shannon told them. "Have you seen it?"

The narwhals bounced up and down in the water, looking very excited. "We think so! We think so!" they all yelled in their tiny voices.

"Not far from here are two strange green creatures," one of the narwhals explained. "They've got flappy black feet."

"Flappy black feet!" the others repeated.

"And they're guarding a big white pearl," another added.

"A BIG WHITE PEARL!" shouted all the narwhals together.

"They were over there by a tall, pointy rock, next to the coral reef," one narwhal explained.

"Over there, over there!" chorused the

others.

"Thank you, my dears," Shannon said with a smile. "Come on, girls."

She swam off at speed, and Kirsty and Rachel followed, pausing only to wave at the narwhals, who were swimming up and down in a frenzy of excitement.

It didn't take long to find the rock the narwhals had mentioned. Cautiously Shannon and the girls peeped out from behind it.

"There they are," Shannon whispered.

"And there's the
Moon Pearl!"

Two goblins were
playing catch
with a big, creamy-
white pearl.
Kirsty caught her breath in wonder,
watching the pearl shimmer in the
turquoise water as the goblins tossed it
back and forth.

"It's not fair!" one of the goblins
moaned. "We're stuck down here,
guarding the Moon
Pearl, while
everyone else is
surfing."

"Yes, and
two new guards
were supposed

to come and take over after half an hour," the other goblin grumbled. "But nobody's turned up!"

Shannon grinned at Rachel and Kirsty. "There are only two of them," she whispered. "This is our chance to get the pearl. But how?"

Rachel thought for a moment. "Maybe we could sneak over to the goblins and grab the pearl when it's in mid-air," she suggested. "Like in a game of piggy-in-the-middle."

Kirsty nodded. "There's coral and clumps of seaweed to hide behind," she said eagerly. "Let's give it a try."

The three of them swam silently from behind the rock to a boulder covered with colourful sea anemones. Then they slipped through the gap between two large pieces of coral and

hid behind a clump of seaweed. They were very close to the goblins now.

Anxiously, they all peered through the seaweed to see if the goblins had spotted them, but they were still throwing the pearl to and fro.

"OK, we're right between the goblins here," Shannon whispered. "Who's going to try to grab the pearl?"

"Rachel, you're good at ball games," said Kirsty.

"I'll have a go," Rachel agreed bravely.

They all waited as one of the goblins prepared to throw the pearl back to the other.

"Now, Rachel!" Shannon said.

Rachel soared upwards from behind the seaweed at the very moment that

the goblin tossed the pearl. As it flew through the air, Rachel swam forward, stretching out her arms to grab it.

Kirsty held her breath as she watched. Would Rachel be able to reach the pearl before the goblins realised what was going on?

Chapter Fourteen
Narwhals Save the Day

Rachel felt her fingertips brush the surface of the pearl, but it was too high for her to catch. "Oh, no!" she groaned as the pearl flew over her head.

"It's those dratted fairies!" yelled the goblin who'd thrown the pearl.

With a determined look on his face,

the other goblin zoomed upwards with
the help of his flippers and snatched the
pearl before Rachel could try to grab
it again.

"Now, run away!" the first goblin
shouted. "Run away!"

The two goblins shot off, propelling
themselves at top speed with their huge
magic flippers. Quickly, Shannon and
Kirsty flew to join Rachel.

144

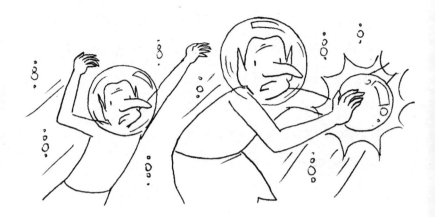

"After them!" Shannon gasped. The three fairies swam swiftly after the goblins.

They raced along the coral reef,
passing shoals of fish and even a very
surprised-looking turtle. But the
goblins, with the help of their
magic flippers, were just
too quick to catch.

"It's no good,"
Shannon

panted as the goblins disappeared from sight. "They're too fast." She stopped and glanced at Rachel and Kirsty in dismay. "How are we ever going to get the Moon Pearl back?"

Suddenly they heard a chorus of tiny voices say, "We can help! We can help!" The Hawaiian narwhals were back, bobbing through the water in a long line. "Let us help you catch the goblins!"

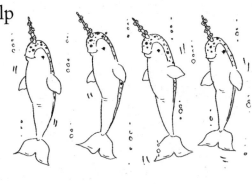

"You can ride on our backs," one suggested.

"Yes, you can ride on our backs!" the others agreed.

Shannon smiled. "That's very kind," she said gently, "but I don't think you'll be fast enough."

"We will, we will," the narwhals chorused. "We've been practising. Now we're extra fast!"

Shannon turned to Rachel and Kirsty. "In that case, climb aboard, girls," she laughed.

Rachel and Kirsty each jumped on to the back of a narwhal, and Shannon did the same.

"Hold on! Hold tight!" the narwhals shouted and zoomed away.

"They are fast!" Kirsty gasped, clinging to her narwhal's neck as they shot through the water at great speed.

The narwhals were extremely agile, dodging neatly around obstacles like rocks and shells and racing in and out of coral arches.

"There are the goblins," Rachel said, as she caught a glimpse of them swimming just ahead. "We're catching them up!"

How are we ever going to get the pearl away from them? Kirsty wondered as her narwhal whizzed past a clump of feathery seaweed. But as she glanced at the long fronds waving in the water, she suddenly had an idea. "Maybe we could tie the goblins up with seaweed!"

"Good idea!" Shannon cried. She immediately raised her wand and, with

a burst of fairy magic, knotted together some long strands of seaweed.

"Rachel, you take one end of the seaweed rope," Shannon instructed, "and if your narwhal keeps still when we get near the goblins, Kirsty and I can tie the goblins up."

"Yes, keep still, keep still," Rachel's narwhal repeated, nodding his little head.

Quietly, Rachel, Kirsty, Shannon and the narwhals sneaked up behind the goblins.

"Now, everyone except Rachel and her narwhal, whizz round and round the goblins," Shannon whispered.

All the narwhals darted forwards, except for Rachel's, who stayed very still. Rachel hung on to one end of the rope, while Kirsty and Shannon held the rest of it.

"Hurrah!" the narwhals yelled excitedly as they swam around the goblins at top speed. "Round and round and round we go!"

Chapter Fifteen
The Tide Turns

The goblins' eyes almost popped out of their heads when they saw Kirsty, Shannon and the narwhals racing around them.

"It's those fairies again!" one of them yelled. "Run for it!"

But before they could move, the

seaweed rope tightened around them,
stopping them in their tracks. The
goblins cried out with rage as another
and then another length of the seaweed
rope tied them up in knots.

"Help!" the goblins shrieked.

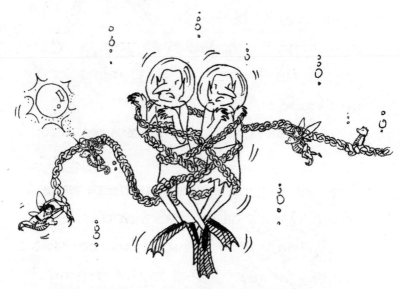

Rachel, Kirsty and Shannon rode their
narwhals over to the goblins and took
the Moon Pearl right out of their hands.

The goblins scowled at them.

"When we let go of the rope, it will take you a little while to free yourselves," Shannon told them. "That will give you time to think about how naughty you've been."

"Horrible fairy!" the goblins muttered rudely, poking their tongues out at her.

Shannon quickly touched her wand to the creamy surface of the Moon Pearl, and it instantly shrank to its Fairyland size.

"Thank you, my friends," Shannon called to the narwhals, who were still dancing happily around the goblins. She waved her wand, showering herself and Rachel and Kirsty with sparkles. "See you again soon!"

"Bye-bye! Bye-bye!" the narwhals chorused.

The next moment, the girls found themselves whizzing through the air as Shannon's magic whisked them up and out of the sea.

"I think the goblins will rush

back to Jack Frost now to tell him they've lost the Moon Pearl," Shannon called to Rachel and Kirsty. "Which means that hopefully they'll leave Hawaii before any humans spot them." She glanced down and pointed with her wand. "Look, girls!"

Rachel and Kirsty gazed down and saw that they were now flying over Fairyland.

Rachel gasped. "Look at the river!" she cried.

The twisting river that wound its way through the green fairy

meadows had burst
its banks. Lots of the
toadstool houses were
already surrounded
by water.

"Fairyland is even
more badly affected than
the human world, because
everything's so
small," Shannon
said.

Kirsty and
Rachel were
dismayed
to see

that the pink and white Fairyland Palace
was also flooded.

Shannon swooped down and in
through the window of the Royal
Observatory, with the girls right
behind her.

Inside, they found King

Oberon, Queen Titania and Cedric the
Royal Astronomer.

"Ah, we knew you wouldn't let us
down," King Oberon declared with a
smile, as Shannon handed the Moon
Pearl to Cedric.

Cedric beamed as he hurried over to
the crystal box. He placed the Moon
Pearl next to the Dawn and Twilight
Pearls, and all three shimmered with a
magical glow.

"Come and look out
of the window,
girls," said Queen
Titania.

Kirsty and
Rachel ran to see.

"The water level's
going down already!"

Kirsty cried, relieved.

They all watched happily as fairies began popping out of their little houses, cheering and clapping.

"This calls for a celebration!" Queen Titania proclaimed. "And what better way to celebrate than to finish our luau?"

Shannon and the girls glanced at each other in delight as the Queen hurried off to organise the party.

Soon the luau was in full swing on the beach again. Kirsty, Rachel and all the fairies joined in the singing and dancing. The ocean was full of happy creatures bobbing on the surface, including their narwhal friends. Even the baby Hawaiian narwhals had made the trip to celebrate with them.

"This is the best party ever," Rachel sighed happily as the sun began to set on Fairyland.

Just then, Queen Titania called for attention. "We want to thank our great friends, the narwhals, for helping to save Fairyland."

The narwhals bobbing in the sea looked at each other in delight, and Kirsty thought she saw one of the baby

Hawaiian narwhals blushing.

"And we must also thank Shannon the Ocean Fairy, and of course Rachel and Kirsty," Queen Titania continued. "Without them, Jack Frost would still have our precious pearls."

The queen pointed her wand at Rachel and Kirsty, and a shower of fairy dust fell gently around them. When it cleared, the girls gasped with delight.

They were each wearing a beautiful gold ring set with a rosy pink pearl that looked just like the Dawn Pearl.

"Thank you," Rachel and Kirsty said gratefully.

"And now you must be getting home," said the queen.

Shannon gave the girls a big hug. "Goodbye," she cried.

"Goodbye!" Rachel and Kirsty called, waving to all their friends as the Queen's magic sent them whizzing home.

A few seconds later, the girls found themselves on the beach near Gran's

house, and back to their normal size.

"Wasn't that an amazing adventure?" Kirsty said happily as they went up the cliff steps towards the house.

"Oh, yes," Rachel agreed, admiring her beautiful ring. "Our fairy adventures are always amazing. But this one under the sea was extra special!"

The End

Now it's time for Kirsty and
Rachel to help ...

Evelyn the
Mermicorn Fairy

Read on for a sneak peek ...

"I love listening to the rain beating
on the window," said Rachel Walker.
"Especially when it's so cosy inside."

She snuggled deeper into her favourite
armchair and gazed into the flickering
flames of the fire. Her best friend, Kirsty
Tate, put down the pattern she was
stitching.

"Me too," she said.

Kirsty was spending the last week of
the summer holidays at Rachel's house
in Tippington. Although they went to

different schools, they saw each other as often as they could. They always had the best fun when they were together, and they often shared secret, magical adventures with their fairy friends.

The sitting room door opened and Rachel's dad popped his head around it.

"Anyone for hot chocolate?" he asked.

"Yes please," said the girls together.

"With whipped cream and sprinkles?" Rachel added.

"Of course," said Mr Walker. "Maybe it'll make up for not being able to go pebble collecting on the beach. What did you want the pebbles for?"

"We were going to paint inspiring pictures and messages on them, and then put them back on the beach for other people to find," Kirsty explained.

"But it's OK," said Rachel. "We found

something else crafty to do instead."

Her dad looked at the cross-stitch patterns they were holding. Kirsty was working on a turquoise mermaid with golden hair, and Rachel was stitching a snow-white unicorn.

"Those look complicated," he said.

"Yes, but it'll be a great feeling when they're finished," said Kirsty.

Mr Walker went to make the hot chocolate, and the girls carried on stitching.

"What's your favourite, mermaids or unicorns?" asked Rachel.

"I don't think I can choose," said Kirsty. "After all, we've met them both on our adventures, and they were just as magical and inspiring as each other."

Just then, they heard a tiny, tinkling giggle. The girls exchanged a surprised glance.

"That sounded exactly like a fairy," said Rachel.

There was another bell-like giggle, and the girls jumped to their feet.

"Where are you?" Kirsty asked.

Then Rachel noticed that her dark hair was sprinkled with sparkling fairy dust. Kirsty saw the same thing on Rachel's hair. They both looked up at the same time, and laughed out loud.

A chestnut-haired fairy was waving at them from the top of the round glass light pendant. She slid down it with a whoop and turned somersaults through the air, landing on the sofa arm with a bounce. She was wearing a shimmering, glittery blue skirt and a matching denim jacket.

"Hello," she said. "I'm Evelyn the Mermicorn Fairy."

"Hello, Evelyn," said Rachel, kneeling down in front of her. "What has brought you to my sitting room?"

"And what's a mermicorn?" Kirsty added.

"Exactly what it sounds like," said Evelyn with a smile. "It's the rarest, most magical creature in all of Fairyland – half mermaid and half unicorn."

"Oh, it sounds wonderful," said Kirsty in a whisper. "I wish I could see one."

"We only see them once a year," said Evelyn. "We always celebrate their visit with the Mermicorn Festival. That's why I'm here. Would you like to come and enjoy the festival with me?"

Rachel and Kirsty squealed in excitement.

"We'd love to," said Kirsty.

"Then it's time to go to Fairyland,"

said Evelyn. She opened her hand, and the girls saw that she was holding a little pile of sparkling fairy dust.

"Don't you have a wand?" asked Rachel.

Read Evelyn the Mermicorn Fairy to find out what adventures are in store for Kirsty and Rachel!

Calling all parents, carers and teachers!
The Rainbow Magic fairies are here to help
your child enter the magical world of reading.
Whatever reading stage they are at, there's
a Rainbow Magic book for everyone!
Here is Lydia the Reading Fairy's guide to
supporting your child's journey at all levels.

Starting Out

Our Rainbow Magic Beginner Readers are perfect for first-time readers who are just beginning to develop reading skills and confidence. Approved by teachers, they contain a full range of educational levelling, as well as lively full-colour illustrations.

(1)

Developing Readers

Rainbow Magic Early Readers contain longer stories and wider vocabulary for building stamina and growing confidence. These are adaptations of our most popular Rainbow Magic stories, specially developed for younger readers in conjunction with an Early Years reading consultant, with full-colour illustrations.

(2)

Going Solo

The Rainbow Magic chapter books - a mixture of series and one-off specials - contain accessible writing to encourage your child to venture into reading independently. These highly collectible and much-loved magical stories inspire a love of reading to last a lifetime.

(3)

www.rainbowmagicbooks.co.uk

"Rainbow Magic got my daughter reading chapter books. Great sparkly covers, cute fairies and traditional stories full of magic that she found impossible to put down" - Mother of Edie (6 years)

"Florence LOVES the Rainbow Magic books. She really enjoys reading now" - Mother of Florence (6 years)

The Rainbow Magic Reading Challenge

Well done, fairy friend – you have completed the book!
This book was worth 10 points.

See how far you have climbed on the
Reading Rainbow opposite.

The more books you read, the more points you will get,
and the closer you will be to becoming a Fairy Princess!

Do you want your own Reading Rainbow?
1. Cut out the coin below
2. Go to the Rainbow Magic website
3. Download and print out your poster
4. Add your coin and climb up the Reading Rainbow!

There's all this and lots more at
www.rainbowmagicbooks.co.uk

You'll find activities, competitions, stories, a special
newsletter and complete profiles of all the
Rainbow Magic fairies. Find a fairy with your name!